Green Light Readers

For the new reader who's ready to GO!

Amazing adventures await every young child who is eager to read.

Green Light Readers encourage children to explore, to imagine, and to grow through books. Created for beginning readers at two levels of skill, these lively illustrated stories have been carefully developed to reinforce reading basics taught at school and to make reading a fun and rewarding experience for children and grown-ups to share outside the classroom.

The grades and ages within each skill level are general guidelines only, and books included in both levels may feature any or all of the bulleted characteristics. When choosing a book for a new reader, remember that every child progresses at his or her own pace—be patient and supportive as the magic of reading takes hold.

❶ Buckle up!

Kindergarten–Grade 1: Developing reading skills, ages 5–7

- Short, simple stories • Fully illustrated • Familiar objects and situations
- Playful rhythms • Spoken language patterns of children
- Rhymes and repeated phrases • Strong link between text and art

2 Start the engine!

Grades 1–2: Reading with help, ages 6–8

- Longer stories, including nonfiction • Short chapters
- Generously illustrated • Less-familiar situations
- More fully developed characters • Creative language, including dialogue
- More subtle link between text and art

Green Light Readers incorporate characteristics detailed in the Reading Recovery model used by educators to assess the readability of texts through the end of first grade. Guidelines for reading levels for these readers have been developed with assistance from Mary Lou Meerson. An educational consultant, Ms. Meerson has been a classroom teacher, a language arts coordinator, an elementary school principal, and a university professor.

Published in collaboration with Harcourt School Publishers

What Day
Is It?

What Day Is It?

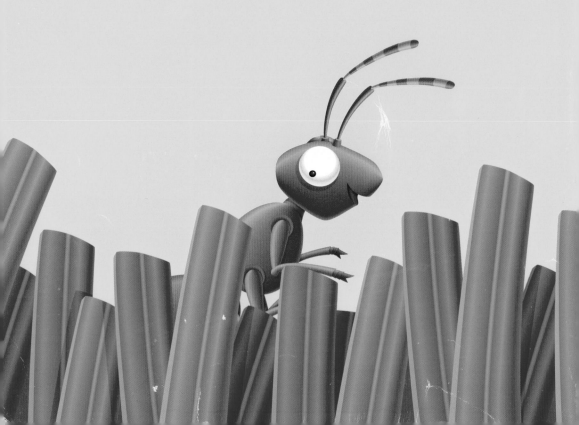

Patti Trimble

Illustrated by Daniel Moreton

Green Light Readers
Harcourt, Inc.
San Diego   New York   London

First Green Light Readers edition 2000
Green Light Readers is a registered trademark of Harcourt, Inc.

Library of Congress Cataloging-in-Publication Data
Trimble, Patti.
What day is it?/Patti Trimble; illustrated by Daniel Moreton.
—1st Green Light Readers ed.
p. cm.
"Green Light Readers."
Summary: Gil the ant mistakenly believes that all
of his friends have forgotten his birthday.
[1. Birthdays—Fiction. 2. Ants—Fiction.] I. Moreton, Daniel, ill. II. Title.
PZ7.T73525Wh 2000
[E]—dc21   99-6816
ISBN 0-15-202500-6
ISBN 0-15-202506-5 (pb)

A C E G H F D B

A C E G H F D B (pb)

Gil was glad.
"This is my big day!"

Gil saw Ann.
"Ann! What day is it?"

"It's Monday," said Ann.

Gil was sad.
"Ann forgot my big day."

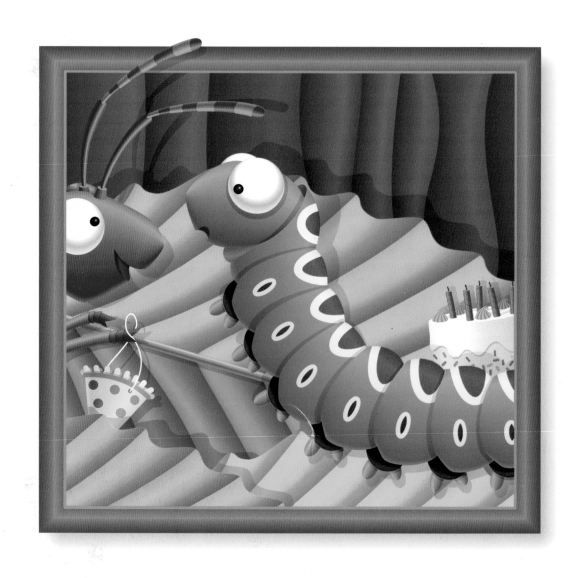

Gil saw Todd.
"Todd! What day is it?"

"It's Monday," said Todd.

"Ann and Todd forgot that
this is my big day!"

Gil was so sad.

"My friends forgot," he said.
"It's my birthday, and they missed it."

"We did not miss it!
Happy birthday, Gil!"

"Thank you," said Gil.
"This is a surprise!"

Meet the Illustrator

Daniel Moreton loved listening to his grandmother's stories when he was a child. They made him want to write stories and books of his own. He creates pictures for his books, too. He uses a computer to draw them, just as he did for this story about Gil the ant. He hopes his stories inspire you to write stories of your own!

Look for these other Green Light Readers
in affordably priced paperbacks and hardcovers!

<table>
<tr><td>

Level 1/Kindergarten–Grade 1

Big Brown Bear
David McPhail

Cloudy Day/Sunny Day
Donald Crews

Down on the Farm
Rita Lascaro

Just Clowning Around
Steven MacDonald
Illustrated by David McPhail

Popcorn
Alex Moran
Illustrated by Betsy Everitt

Six Silly Foxes
Alex Moran
Illustrated by Keith Baker

Sometimes
Keith Baker

The Tapping Tale
Judy Giglio
Illustrated by Joe Cepeda

What I See
Holly Keller

</td><td>

Level 2/Grades 1–2

Animals on the Go
Jessica Brett
Illustrated by Richard Cowdrey

A Bed Full of Cats
Holly Keller

Catch Me If You Can!
Bernard Most

The Chick That Wouldn't Hatch
Claire Daniel
Illustrated by Lisa Campbell Ernst

Digger Pig and the Turnip
Caron Lee Cohen
Illustrated by Christopher Denise

The Fox and the Stork
Gerald McDermott

Get That Pest!
Erin Douglas
Illustrated by Wong Herbert Lee

I Wonder
Tana Hoban

Shoe Town
Janet Stevens and Susan Stevens Crummel
Illustrated by Janet Stevens

The Very Boastful Kangaroo
Bernard Most

</td></tr>
</table>

Green Light Readers is a registered trademark of Harcourt, Inc.

Green Light Readers
For the new reader who's ready to GO!